# I'M NOT MOVING!

*Story by* PENELOPE JONES
*Pictures by* AMY AITKEN

BRADBURY PRESS / SCARSDALE, NEW YORK

J
J

The text of this book is set in 16 pt. Caledonia. The illustrations are pencil and watercolor wash reproduced in full color.

Library of Congress Cataloging in Publication Data
Jones, Penelope, 1938–
I'm not moving!
Summary: Five-year-old Emmy is determined that she won't move with her family and scouts the neighborhood for someone to take her in.

1. Moving, Household – Fiction     I. Aitken, Amy.
II. Title.
PZ7.J7243Im  [E]       79-13062
ISBN 0-87888-156-5

*To my father, Gikas Critikos — P.J.*

*To Mary Fertick — A.A.*

My father, my mother, my brothers,
and even my dog are moving to another house far away,
but I'm not moving. I don't want to move. I decided.

I want to stay here.

My digging hole is here. I can't leave my digging hole.
My father helped me dig my digging hole
with a big shovel.

My digging hole is so deep that I can get in it
and nobody can see me.

When I fill it up with water, it takes a real, real, real long time.

I'll never leave my digging hole. I can't. I won't!
I'm going to stay right here. . . . Somewhere.
I'll find a place somewhere. Where?

The Morrises. Yes.
Mrs. Morris makes gingerbread men
and ice cream in an ice cream machine.
That's where I'll stay!

"Mrs. Morris, can I stay with you?" I asked.
She let me come in and watch her cook.

"What are you cooking?" I asked.
"Brown rice for dinner," she said.
She lifted the lid and showed it to me.

I decided to leave.

I walked down my street to Babby's house. Babby has
a beautiful thing over her bed like a princess.
That's where I'll stay!
"Babby, can I stay with you?" I asked.

We went to her room to play house.
I let her be the mother first. I was the sick child
who lay on the bed. I put my face in her pillow.
It had a funny smell.
I pretended to get well real fast.

As I walked down Babby's driveway,
Mr. Feldberg called to me.
"Hi there, Emmy," he said.
Mr. Feldberg was nice. He let me and my brothers
pull carrots from his garden and wash them
with his hose and eat them outdoors.
"Can I stay with you, Mr. Feldberg?" I asked.
"For a while," he said. "I've a great deal of weeding to do.
Say, how would you like to help?" he asked.

I pulled weeds and weeds and weeds...

. . . but no carrots.
"I think I have to go," I said to Mr. Feldberg.
Where? Where? Where can I stay? I thought
as I headed along.
The Robinsons? Yes. They don't have children.
They can do things with me all the time.

"Can I stay with you, Mrs. Robinson?" I asked
when she opened the door.
"Emmy! What a pleasant surprise!
Come in and sit down," she said.

I walked in the house and went to a chair.
Lily, her big white cat, was already there.
"Nice Lily," I said, as I reached for her fur.

"Don't touch the cat, my dear," Mrs. Robinson said.
Lily lept from the chair and stretched out her claws.
She opened her mouth and showed me her teeth.
"I'm supposed to go home right now,
Mrs. Robinson," I said.

I stood in my street and I looked all around.
There's no place good to stay.
I don't care. I'm not moving.
I'll never leave my digging hole anyway.
Never! never! never!

I'll dig my digging hole so deep and so big.
I'll even stay in my digging hole.
I'll sleep in my digging hole. I'll eat in my digging hole.
That's what I'm going to do!

I went right home to my hole to dig.
I dug

and I dug

and I dug.

I smelled a delicious dinner smell.
I felt too hungry to dig anymore.

"Em!" I heard my father call. "Emmy!"
I began to dig again.

"I knew I'd find you here," my father said.
"The hamburgers are ready to come off the grill."
I stopped digging.
My mother came out to my hole too.

"Well, Miss Em," she asked,
"what should we wash for dinner? You or the mud?"
"ME!" I said.
My mother always makes me laugh.

"You'd better save that digging arm
for our new backyard," my father said.
"I bet you and I can dig an even better hole."

I put my shovel down.
"A better hole?" I asked.
"Sure," my father said.
"I know where I want to stay," I said.
"Where?" my father asked.

"With you!"